THE CROW and MRS. GADDY

by Wilson Gage

pictures by Marylin Hafner

SCHOLASTIC INC.

New York Toronto London Auckland Sydney

ISBN 0-590-33643-6

12 11 10 9 8 7 6 5 4 3 2 1   11   5 6 7 8 9/8 0/9

Printed in the U.S.A.   28

Mrs. Gaddy was a farmer.

She grew lots of corn

to feed her cow and her mule

and her chickens.

One spring day Mrs. Gaddy

planted her corn.

She made furrows in the earth

and dropped in grains of corn.

Then she waited

for the corn to sprout.

She waited and waited.

Many days passed.

Nothing happened.

"Tarnation!" cried Mrs. Gaddy.

"I believe a bad crow

has eaten all my grains of corn.

Well, I know what to do

about that!"

Once again Mrs. Gaddy
made furrows in the earth.
But this time she did not
drop in grains of corn.
Instead she dropped in
round white pebbles.

Mrs. Gaddy went back
to her house.
It was Monday
and she had to do her washing.
Sure enough
a crow flew down from a tree.
He began to eat the pebbles.
"Ugh!" said the crow.
"These are not grains of corn!
Oh, I feel terrible!
What a mean woman.
I will get even with her!"

Mrs. Gaddy hung her clothes
on a line to dry.
"What a fine sunny day," she said.
"Now I must bake some bread."
She went into the house.

And that crow flew up
and pulled all the clothespins
from the line.

Plop! Plop! Plop!
All the clean clothes
fell down into the dirt.

Mrs. Gaddy looked out the window.

'Oh, my stars and garters!"

she cried.

"Look what that bad crow has done!

Now I will have to wash

all my clothes again."

But Mrs. Gaddy did not

wash the clothes again.

Instead she baked gingerbread.

She put in lots and lots of ginger.

She also put in lots of salt

and some soap powder and pepper.

When the gingerbread was baked,
Mrs. Gaddy put it
on the windowsill to cool.

"There," she said. "I will have
gingerbread for my supper."

The crow saw the pan on the sill.

By and by he flew down

and took a big bite of gingerbread.

"Oooh! Blah!" croaked the crow.

"What awful gingerbread!

It tastes like salt.

It tastes like soap.

That mean woman has played

another trick on me.

But I will get even with her!"

He looked all around.
Mrs. Gaddy's knitting
was lying on a table.
The crow grabbed the yarn
and pulled and pulled
and pulled.

All the stitches came undone.
The knitting was just a pile
of tangled yarn.

"Oh, my stars and stockings!"
yelled Mrs. Gaddy. "That bad crow
has unknitted my sweater!
Well, I will teach him a good lesson."
Mrs. Gaddy went to town.
She bought some balloons.
That night she blew them up.
In the dark she went outside
and tied the balloons
all over her apple tree.

The next morning Mrs. Gaddy
looked out her window.
"My, what lovely apples!"
she shouted.
"I hope that crow
doesn't peck them."

Right away the crow flew
to the apple tree.
He gave one of the balloons
a really hard peck.
POW! went the balloon.
"Ow!" went the crow. "That hurt.
What a mean woman.
But I can get even with her."

Mrs. Gaddy went to the barn
to milk her cow.
The crow found a big black beetle.
Mrs. Gaddy came out of the barn
with a pail of milk.

The crow flew over
and dropped the beetle
right into the milk.
Mrs. Gaddy's good fresh milk
was spoiled.
She was mad.
"But I will teach that crow
a lesson," she said.

Every day Mrs. Gaddy played
a new trick on the crow.
Every day the crow played
a new trick on Mrs. Gaddy.
The crow was so busy
he did not have time
to find a wife.
He did not have time
to raise a family.

Mrs. Gaddy was so busy
she did not have time
to work in her garden.

She did not have time
to keep her house
clean and tidy.

One day she went into her garden
to get some beans for supper.
"Oh, bless my big toe!"
cried Mrs. Gaddy.
"What a horrible mess!
Look at all those weeds!
Look at all those bugs
eating my tomatoes!"
She worked and worked.
She hoed and weeded and raked.

At the end of the day
she was very tired.
She went right to bed
and slept and slept.
The sun rose the next morning

and still Mrs. Gaddy was sleeping.
The crow looked in her window
to see what was the matter.
Mrs. Gaddy was sleeping.
Her glasses were on
the table beside her bed.

"Goody," said the crow.

"I will fix that old woman.

I will steal her glasses!"

He flew in the window

and picked up the glasses.

Mrs. Gaddy woke up.

She sat up in bed.

"Who's there?" she cried.

The crow was scared.

Instead of flying out the window

he flew down the stairs.

"Who's there?"

Mrs. Gaddy yelled again.

"Where are my glasses?"

Maybe I left my glasses
in the kitchen,
thought Mrs. Gaddy.
She put on her slippers
and went down the stairs.

She could barely see.
She went into the kitchen.
The crow was perched
on the stove.

"Oh, drat and drat!"
  cried Mrs. Gaddy.
"My kitchen is a mess.
  I have wasted so much time
  with that bad crow.
  I should have been scrubbing
  my kitchen and tending my garden.
  Oh, look at that big black smut
  on my nice stove!"
  Mrs. Gaddy grabbed
  her feather duster.

She tried to dust the crow
off the stove.
"What a big smut!" she cried.
"I can't dust it away."

She grabbed a pail
of soap and water.
She threw it on the crow.
"That horrid smut!
It won't go away,"
shouted Mrs. Gaddy.

She picked up the firetongs
and snapped them at the smut.
The tongs closed over
the crow's tail feathers.
"What a big smut,"
said Mrs. Gaddy.
She opened the door
and threw the crow outside.

The crow landed in a rosebush.

"What a mean woman,"

he croaked.

"She is trying to kill me.

First she nearly

tickled me to death.

Then she tried to drown me.

And now I am stuck

in this rosebush.

I don't think I will try

to get even with her again."

Mrs. Gaddy went back upstairs.
She got dressed
and put on her best hat.
She was going to town
to buy some new glasses.
"I am a stupid woman," she cried.
"I was so dumb to waste my time
teaching that crow a lesson.

Now my house is dirty
and my garden is full of weeds.
I should have made a scarecrow
instead of baking gingerbread
with soap in it."

Mrs. Gaddy began to laugh.
"Ha! Ha! Ha! It was so funny
when he ate that awful stuff.
Next time I will bake a pie
filled with hot peppers.
I bet that will teach him!"

The crow climbed
out of the rosebush.
He was all scratched up.
His feathers were so wet
he could not fly.

He had no wife or children
to comfort him.
"I have been really dumb,"
said the crow.
"I have wasted all summer
getting even with that mean woman.
I wasted my time finding
a beetle to drop in her milk."

The crow scratched his head.

"Ho! Ho! Ho!" he croaked.

"That really made me laugh.
Next time I will find
a snake to drop in her milk pail!
I bet that will fix her."

Just then the crow heard Mrs. Gaddy.

She was laughing. "Ha! Ha! Ha!"

"Oh, oh," said the crow.

"I bet that mean woman
has thought of a really awful trick
to play on me.

I wonder what it is.

I don't think I'll wait to see."

And he dried his feathers

and flew away to look for a snake.

Just in case.

WILSON GAGE is the pen name of Mary Q. Steele, who has written many popular books for children. As Wilson Gage, she is the author of another tale about Mrs. Gaddy and an unwanted house guest, *Mrs. Gaddy and the Ghost*, and two ALA Notable Books, *Squash Pie* and *Down in the Boondocks*. Under her own name, she is the author of *Journey Outside*, a Newbery Honor Book, as well as many other books including *Wish Come True*, *The Life (and Death) of Sarah Elizabeth Harwood*, and *Because of the Sand Witches There*.
Born and raised in Tennessee,
Ms. Steele lives there today
in Chattanooga.

MARYLIN HAFNER studied at Pratt Institute and the School of Visual Arts in New York City, and in her early career did advertising illustration and fabric design. She continues to do editorial illustrations for leading magazines and has illustrated many distinguished books, including *Mrs. Gaddy and the Ghost* by Wilson Gage, *Mind Your Manners* by Peggy Parish, *It's Halloween* by Jack Prelutsky, *Camp KeeWee's Secret Weapon* and *Jenny and the Tennis Nut* by Janet Schulman, and *Big Sisters Are Bad Witches* by Morse Hamilton.
Ms. Hafner lives in Cambridge, Massachusetts.